WINTER TOYS

*Poems by
Katherine Soniat*

GreenTower Press
Maryville, Missouri

Acknowledgments

Grateful acknowledgment is given to the following periodicals in whose pages these poems originally appeared:

The Georgia Review, "Mardi Gras Reverie"; *The Greensboro Review*, "Think About It"; *The Kenyon Review*, "Distance and Design"; *The Laurel Review*, "Lightning Rods"; *The Malahat Review*, "Rabbit, Looking for Home"; *Modern Poetry Studies*, "Breath on the Mirror"; *The Nation*, "A Comparable Season"; *New Letters*, "Winter Toys"; *The North American Review*, "October"; *Poetry*, "Lighthouse Telephone"; *Present Tense*, "Alpha" (previously titled "Reporting Back: The Weather"); *The Seneca Review*, "The Future"; *The Southern Review*, "Santa Rosa Island"; *Yarrow*, "The Pascagoula Fishermen"; *The Yale Review*, "Learning in Time."

Cover design & Typesetting by Michael Annis / Typography Photo by Cathyrn Hankla

Financial assistance for this project has been provided by the Missouri Arts Council, a State Agency.

Published by GreenTower Press, Department of English, Northwest Missouri State University, Maryville, Missouri 64468. Individual copies: $4, plus 50¢ postage. Make checks payable to NWMSU/GreenTower Press.

ISBN: 0-9616467-3-X
Copyright © 1989 by Katherine Soniat
All rights reserved
Printed and bound in the United States of America
First Edition

For my father

CONTENTS

Winter Toys 7
Alpha 9
Record Catch: The Pascagoula Fishermen 10
The Future 11
Santa Rosa Island 12
Lightning Rods 13
Strange Music 14
Oranges and Rum at Noon 15
Lessons 16
Breath on the Mirror 17
October 18
Think About It 20
Barncoming 22
To the Top of the Hill 23
Lighthouse Telephone 24
Summer Tea 26
A Comparable Season 28
A Southern Retrospective:
   Portraits from a Private Collection 29
Learning in Time 31
Mardi Gras Reverie 32
Rabbit, Looking for Home 33
Janus in Autumn 34
Distance and Design 35
Rembrandt's Vanities 36
Short Street 38
Crivelli's Pietà Angel 39
Rose Cloth Tattering
   from the Barbed Wire 41

Winter Toys

Winter, and my father
steamed his gray destroyer straight for Cyprus,
deep into what they called the Cold War,

and in his wake gifts arrived —
a gold charm of a gondola from Venice,
a peasant marionette from Genoa —

while in Sunday school, I watched
the wall-map unfold with the cedars of Lebanon,
the Mediterranean blue under the galleys

of early sailing men. Full-moon nights,
my mother would pull down photos
of the *USS South Dakota*, that battleship

she used as memory: "There, on the deck,
that's you in a christening dress," she smiled,
and was far away from me on those nights.

I lived inside the gestures and red enamel
smile of my lady marionette. She danced
her own string quartet, two arms, two legs

flying in time to *Genoa, Genoa*. With a shake
of my bracelet charm, I imagined a rocking gondola
making headway in a world I thought

Jesus would love to take long, watery walks in,
while somewhere to the east, my father in dress whites

wandered lost in evergreens — all of us feeling

lost, as my marionette tapped
her toes, nodding yes
to any stretch of the imagination.

Alpha

Wind. Rain. And somewhere a threat
lifts off the page of a yellowed
almanac. The curtains sail
out the window like the underwater
hair of Norse women, their drowned

faces flashing. The sea reclaims
the trees, tosses up her Vikings
to prowl as overlords on this balcony.
They lay open the sky with light,
thunder of lost continents on the rise.

On a back road, a woman closes a book,
opens the shade on daybreak
and the neighbor's house. Street lights
blur through the window pane,
globed eyes at the end of an enormous night.

Record Catch:
The Pascagoula Fishermen

Two fishermen, poles up,
bottle beer atilt,
witnessed a severe gap in twilight
as on the pier they squatted, watching
a freighter loosely sealed in fog
wash now and again into view. For moments
the pine-tipped edge of Horn Island
hung at close range, hung clear
as wind rounding the water tower.

All clear and simple
until this interlude with twilight fish
came to a halt when gods or stranger
things from space lifted these two men
for hours into a cosmos where reality,
divinity, and Saturday beer balled into one,
then thumped them down again.

Like eager heretics, reporters
flocked to scan the sky
while the town folk stood back,
way back from the water's edge.
Their fishermen stopped fishing,
drinking, and wished they could stop
dreaming as they started recording
albums, getting it down pat
into a fiction old as any:
the larger-than-life contained,
backed off from the nightprowl.

The Future

A city squared on the horizon
and smoke blowing from chimneys that jut
out of wet, slate rooftops — always this
image arrives, seasonless, from nowhere.
Perhaps it was that November, when alone
at the window, I watched the afternoons
mass themselves, rain washing
down a smoky day. Or maybe this heat

never was mine, and memory got it
backwards in its own territorial way,
insisting *it was me, of course,
I was there*. When indeed it was sundown
for some painter who needed warmth
so much, he crossed from his window
and stroked it in, turning it out
as great clouds of colored smoke
that I saw as mine. But what if

this skyline never was at all.
This smoke could come to nothing more
than the tail-end of need, imagination
drifting off into the future as it slips
from the top of the sky
down.

Santa Rosa Island

Nights, the moon would come
clay-red from this Gulf
as you drifted from window to window

insisting it was the moon
that stole your sleep.
But you'd lost him.

He left you once, twice,
until all that remained
of your Navy man was an outline —

a beach, water, and waves.
You kept handing me photographs
of waves, raising and lowering him

on the deck of his ship.
In the tides you heard
a homecoming, steady, steadfast

as make-believe. Return. And return.
He would not come back.
So the dunes became a map to somewhere

your feet could not get enough of,
a lap you kept to climb into,
homesick as any child.

Lightning Rods

rise in accusation above firehouses
and The American Red Cross

while the town's one doctor
surrounds himself with hypodermics

suspecting disaster in his own
small way. He's heard tales

of cyclones lifting the outskirts
of Bombay and fires that peel back

lives on the Serengeti Plain. There
are no funerals on the plains, only cattle

skulls that flare and vanish
like towns on the desert edge.

Strange Music

Are you the shape I was taught,
the one under the street light
with the luminous after-dark hands
and words like licorice twists?

Mornings in the coffee shop,
you lift the pale cup with your hand,
sounds rattling in your throat.
You never speak. You've never spoken

to me. The moist cakes slip down
in single swallows. You make strange
music and look at me as if I were
nothing, or everything. I watch

your hands rise and you become
implicated. You could fit the picture
of one closer to home — that shadow
of a man, with hands rising out of shadow

who came to breathe in my head
when I was ten. Perhaps, you are
the one in the green Ford that stole
my friend away. I dreamed of her

pushing your silvered car door handle
down and tumbling down a grassy slope
while you sped away. By daylight
she was gone two weeks. Then she was

back in silence. Poor, large,
wordless man, I have saved my friend
from one like you in dozens of darks, and
still I meet you. You divide.

Oranges and Rum at Noon

A radio's violins slip through the air
like heat loose in the palmettos,
the Seagrove Market leaning
wooden and sandy as thirty years ago,
its corner phone still the one phone,
sun deepening the Gulf to that old
clear green. Maybe you are up the road
still, behind the door we slammed
on each other after two weeks too much
vacation at thirteen. Azalea Street
curves on the bluff above the sea,
and the man and woman in our summer
cottage seem here too: oranges,
rum on the porch at noon, and then
the inland lake swimming on their bare skins
all afternoon — and you and I taken in,
thinking lives turn out like that.

Lessons

— for Shelton

On Sundays I would hold your hand
to the summer screen, airy with colors,

hummingbirds beak-deep in fuschia.
I said *hummingbird* with your finger

to my lips, then hummed a rosy
lullaby as we walked out to touch

each crisp little landscape,
starting slow with the hedge.

We picked a wooden basket of dandelions,
blew the sky into stars of thistles.

You huffed like my giant busy at creation.
Now the day is no longer a spray of dandelions

or hummingbirds perfectly suspended,
and only I recall how I grew

dandelions and hummingbirds
with your fingers to my mouth.

Breath on the Mirror

The world is always shaping
new hollows, smoothing old ones,
and we go on trying to fit ourselves
to one another. Little was said
when we lay there, our bodies close.
So many days, that was how we started,
in a room that held space for daybreak
and the few late stars.

But I rose, and it was not
from dream. Wrapping myself in woolens,
I wished you a long, slow sleep.
I wished the clocks would stop,
the birds fall silent in the leaves.
Moving from room to room, I turned
each photograph flat, placed a close
warm breath on every mirror
until I made myself and all
the background disappear.

October

Little brown dog, gone fishing,
paw-deep in autumn sky of the creek —
the minnows are around him,
they tempt like deer flagging
white-tailed through the field.

> For one slow rainy season
> I was made quiet by your body,
> its thickening summer stalk —
> desire and need a tangled beginning.

The dog peers past his own toothiness
quivering on the stream's light.
His minnows are traveling away.
In and out and away. A tongue-lap away.

> That day you looked at me looking
> into you like space under the wet gold
> leaves, the message was about leaving.
> It echoed and left us with closed eyes.

Why do surfaces hold the face
aloft, while minnows swirl truantly
beneath? We're no more than ripply smiles
stretched across the depths.

> Why take your head from my belly?
> Let's turn desire loose,
> or shall we turn it to need,

        make it a cold and twisted thing.
        Bulls cleave to the hillside
        with a bellowing for this.

Water striders play stretch
on the surface but tonight
this glass-bottomed-boat-
of-a-creek will hold the stars,
a beauty long gone as it's seen.

        Under my footsteps, one day,
        twigs snapped, and eight wild turkeys
        gusted with fear from the trees,
        beauty and need set off. I want you
        to hear through my skin.

Quiet, staring water-dog,
these minnows are no trees
to run to, and you'll not eat
this wet covering of sunlight.
It fascinates — the dare of disappearance
behind every move.

Think About It

The ground's a stew of apple-rot,
white meat opening for bees
to stick their faces to.

Sometimes eyes stick out from fields —
the wolfish dog's one ice-blue eye
like chicory at noon, and up the road

a hunter's camouflage glove blows
from one place to the next,
never fitting in. This is the October

I can imagine arriving without me
in it. When I look up from reading,
the corn's a blur of crows, my eyes

blurring to all but the print
about Primroses on page 53:
it is lucidly yellow in old fields

and waste places. So there are places
as wasted as this valley when it's adrift
in fog, and voices herding cattle call out,

unseen. Words meaning only the world's
a cold well, the bluish thunk of apples
dying onto ground. Winter's almost here.

I can feel it happening and want
the cat to be my good omen as she rolls
on concrete in the sun. An old sundial,

my mind ranges to a time of heat
and loss. Suddenly I am lost again
with my mother at the end of a carline

in Havana, castanets and palm fronds
clicking as we walk, not a coin
jangling in her purse. Listen,

why not stop all of this?
Stop. Think about it
or not, the mind will go on

changing like apples
in the sun, like crows
circling a field.

Barncoming

Strange to a mountain home,
we sit with Christmas
while the cat hisses at the snow,

offering it an imperious look.
The fire hisses dampness into smoke,
and I leave breathing deeply

a deepening freeze, wind stripping
the abandoned house up the road,
an axe heaved into the last

piece of wood, as if someone
had drawn in his breath,
deciding suddenly to forget

where he lived. He left
the Chinese kite tethered
to make swipes at the coming-down

white weather. The cows alone
seem easy with recall as they ponder
the way back.

To the Top of the Hill

It was his as a boy,
this Western Flyer with the wet,
red rails. And now he pulls
me, a daughter in her thirties,
to the top of Town Hill,
takes me for the ride of a lifetime,
the life war slipped away from him
as he rocked on the Pacific
and I slept in my mother's bed.

Tonight he says *you first*,
and belly down I lie
on the polished wood.
The moon pales above the sled
loaded with six and a half feet of a father
sprawled atop me, clutching
the guidebar as down the hill
we fly, riddling the years
spread in moonlight.

Lighthouse Telephone

You held your hands to my face
when I was four
and blistering with sun, that broken
boat sputtering finally toward home.
You made a breeze with them,
said they were palm trees
near my window, miles ago, in Key West.

Key West had slipped so easily
away, the salt-spray sun
sinking down in orange, twilight
drifting upon us in a fishing boat
that would not start. The only sound
was waves slapping
the boatside in the wind.

Then the lighthouse came alive,
like one match struck in the dark
and blown out, then another.
You tied a hatchet to your
scarlet bathing suit in the starlight
and swam away. The whole Gulf
swam up to me, floating alone.

The sun rose pale from the water
as I bobbed blocks or miles from you
and that white bone of a lighthouse.
Dozing. Waking. Sleeping.
All around, the Gulf was

endless,
the sun growing high again and yellow.

Until the sky began to drone, and a seaplane
floated out of a cloud. My head
was blister-hot, the sun was spinning
gold, voices swam over me from men
in white uniforms: someone in red
had been swimming in a shallows
of sharks. The day froze

to dead calm. *Luck* was all
I heard one say, as your hand
appeared at the seaplane door.
The boat rocked like a cradle,
my skin went cool with noon.
On a green tide of sharks and luck,
we rode all the way home.

Summer Tea

At first, the shape was a thing —
a blowing bag? hat in the field?
Then she saw the whining coon,
her dogs tossing him like an old
summer doll. Once she had pictured

fear as this — it gloomed windows,
hung in the imaginary trees
making cat-whines as she sat
arranging her doll house, its tiny
folk for August tea.

Now that cry was coming clear,
swift as the knowledge of waking
alone and knowing *alone* is the first
and final private thing. The coon's
whine came clear and she came

with a leash, thrashing two dogs
and a coon, not knowing
just what was being saved, the four
of them swirling before something
brisk and unquestioning on the other side.

Later, she returned to that coon,
dog-crippled, now undergoing men
with their shovel as he hunched
to the ground as if to pull it
up for privacy, one of them

mumbling *rabies* and *go on, hit him.*
You afraid? The man beat slowly.
And the coon's whine slowed
to that windy sound outside
a doll house.

A Comparable Season

The cedar waxwing has fallen
too much in love with the juniper berry
this rough winter, carried
his desire fermenting into spring.
We watch thawed skies fill with plunging
birds as, cross country, the hunter,
sharp as daybreak, goes beyond his limit,
under the few remaining stars.

A Southern Retrospective: Portraits from a Private Collection

At the beginning, no oaks or levees
rise behind a paddle-wheeler.
There is "Henry Durrell III," done up

and framed in 1710. In white knee breeches,
he struts about the South, with a falcon
on his fist and a black boy at his feet

whose white-eyed, worshipful look
is a paradigm — he's the first black slave
painted in America, and perhaps that's the reason

why Henry and his falcon were kept on,
framed for the next century, for a time
when the Civil War was not quite ready

for canvas. Its roots were still sunk
in the cotton field when somebody got busy
painting "The Breakdown," dance of a grinning

black boy, red harmonica honking to his feet.
He must be looking forward to "Sunrise
at Fort Sumter, 1864," hung to the right

of "Portrait of a Gentleman," subject unknown.
He has that saintly, anonymous look
coming from too many benedictions over wine.

But it's almost evening in his South,

and the gentleman seems comfortably
at home — before home disappeared

and the South gave up those cabins
of happy dancing feet it had
a hard time painting into place.

Learning in Time

You read of hospital hallways
crowded like wards,
of peasants, not soldiers, marooned
in a corridor's white light.
You learn the value of eyes
put out, how their dark will bleed
the State. But you are seeing
that hallway, its clock
where the one with his eyes
blown out is lifted by another
to relearn the face of a clock,
while somewhere off in a field
another is tugged from blasted
corn and left on the roadside
mined for sheep and those who tend
the sheep. This is the roadway
that winds to the white hallway
where the hands of one man
hold the hands of another
to the hands of a clock.

Mardi Gras Reverie

It's not the little children
pulled under this mistaken
fairy tale; it's the mothers,
the fathers, great-aunts
and grandmothers. They grow
large as embattled royalty
to play out the Middle Ages
in this low city
where even the next breath
is hard to come by.
They cancel entire centuries
to rule one day, singing praises

to each other and the dust
of passed-down rhinestones.
They whisper of the black torch carrier,
his flambeaux strutting proper,
set to a jungle beat. All this drumming
and tropic firelight sends them groping
back for a sovereign grandfather, porticoes,
white cotton and black men.

Rabbit, Looking for Home

Once he owned my back yard
and more: my black Persian
cat. Her furriness enticed him
to dream of a thickly rabbited earth.
He lusted after cats, any cats,
declared himself a cat to prowl

the world at large. And there
he held a Siamese at bay on a car engine
in range of Sunday bells and patent leather
shoes tapping down the street.
Cat or rabbit, it made no difference,
his heart thumping, his world
turned upside down. He crouched
like a domestic dream gone bad,
not a field or hawk in sight.

All this just to press down,
pelt to soft pelt
and believe in a cane field again
where no Chevrolet holds
furred illusion high
on an engine, origin Detroit.

Janus in Autumn

The hornets enter such a dark
nest, alive with their one great hum.
It's hard to picture each
with strength enough to hang the earth
from this Appalachian Power line —
and something plugged one golden ear
of corn above their entrance, thrust it
into the practical mud daubed up,
then down, the curve of every
invitation and departure.
                                      In late October
the landscape assumes a wrinkled look.
Do you think it's just exhaustion,
that sleepy hornet hum? It makes me
picture cold migrants, and the hornets
stay close as if a tiny trap door kept
thudding, reminding each of home.
When the first freeze empties their black
hallway and the season,
only their gray, waved efforts will remain.

Distance and Design

In those first moments of spring
at Ed's place we spoke of moonlight —
how last night on Highway 64 a moonlit horse
shot out of its pasture and into the man
driving home from a poker game,
his private apocalypse arriving
for the moment when two lives confront
and leave as a single signal.
Who could have imagined such horse-dazzle
at life's end? You said it made you think
of horseblinders, the pure tunnel-vision
of a guy who once sat down next to you
in a diner and proceeded to gobble
your 2 a.m. meatball sandwich as if
you did not exist.
                        Maybe the moon
was loose that night too, tidying up
the strange imbalances that later
I drive home through — a yolky moon
tips over the mountains, and I am
still imagining that plunging horse
when up ahead on the back road
come three jostling rumps.
Peasant skirts shag the gravel
until four hooves appear on each,
and it's three goats prancing the potholed night.
They do not scatter for my horn
but dare the headlights with silvery coats
and windy goatees, those beasts of revelation
lighting out upon the highway.

Rembrandt's Vanities

I
318 years and 14,000 square feet
of flagstone later, the town fathers

are using the self-portraits to identify
your bones mixed into the pauper pit

beneath Amsterdam's Western Church.
Vain little trick you played though,

painting yourself enough beauty
to die behind, enough perfection

to confound a whole line of computers
busily designing you a skull. You,

who coated yourself with hues of apricot
and plum in the fur-dark rooms, go on

vanishing. Lie quiet among those
never born for limelight,

those born to disappear
into history's stone-gray privacy.

II
Today it's enigma they encounter
in your self-portraits' untelling eyes —

the anatomical technicians up against
the crystal ball of an imagination

swirled around the skull. So
they study bones beneath the flagstone

for a possible Rembrandt, seeking
revelation from signs of ingested lead.

Does one of them picture you chewing
a raisin cake, pondering

above the oily glaze of colors —
these men who pick through a dark

of pelvic bones looking for sex,
looking for the right son of a miller?

III
Where lies the skull of the right son
of the right miller? The one that thought

in amber, then purple tint. There's not
one scar or palsied eye to mar his painted

flesh — poor dead beauty makes a mock
of us. Rembrandt, unhonorable man,

makes a mock of our century
turned toward an end.

Short Street

Vapo-Rub is blowing through
my dream, through that green, wooden house,
corner of Fern and Short.
Your Granny is taking her time
dying again, and I arrive routinely
to sit on a stretcher parked outside her window.
The phone keeps ringing
while granddaughters, paired to a room,
doze and grow toward perfume.

Tonight, the stretcher is my task.
I welcome its broad, flat emptiness.
Your white-skinned Granny coughs
at a cat from my old marriage
scratching her window screen.
Wobbly-fleeced and dying,
it thuds to the flower bed.

In this flux of cats and women
shrunk to grandmothers,
my own dead mother arrives,
her forehead calcified to dust.
All the way from Short Street,
they've come to converge like youth
laid out cold in mid-air.

Crivelli's Pietà Angel

Then it was just another spring
of wind and noon-dark weather.
Betrayal or not,
things went on from there.
But this angel's sopped eyes are beyond
consolation, stopped by a brokenness
the living feel about the dead —
a sadness like winter, all there is.
And Crivelli must have known it,
with each gray, each plum daub to the sockets.

*

Once birds arced back and forth
in the cold outside a city,
and slowly departing, I could not see
my hesitation as natural —
the jerking toward death and change
the charm of all that is natural.

*

Suffer in place, angel, like all
who cannot make casual the past.
Today this seeding of birds across the sky
seems the same as years before. It was
winter then, and it is winter now.
But how can I get back to that corner

where the one I left with someone
else becomes someone else?

*

I want what the angel cannot have.
The birds full of new hearts
are dipping over a tangle of iron tracks.
But this angel has no future,
and these birds do not fly out of the past —
unlike all of those expressions
Crivelli must have pondered
before shading history on an angel's face.

Rose Cloth
Tattering from the Barbed Wire

Incinerator cans blaze
in back lots, crackle under the hands
of those who will not be found.
And insist on it. All the glistening
water filling an eye will not call
one back. No one even glances up
from a hand on the shoulder —
is that you?

*

Still we believe a benevolent surf
swells to wash things back.
At night, the wind suggests it,
curling shingles, billowing
screens, changing direction
in the bent trees.

*

Who was it that wandered out the screen door,
then disappeared? One moment, life was
thick as sighs on a night dizzy with mosquitoes.
Then ivy darkened an empty room.
They said the phone rang for days.

*

Now rain sheets before the mountains,
and I want to route maps home,

over islands, the waters in between.
But, thinking back . . .
who left, you or me? You recall
how the trail ended, how abrupt.
I keep holding the shrubs away
over the last footprint
as clouds and sunlight scope the valley,
search for something gone.

*

Tonight, the moon's too giant
and orange for the sky. I lie down
at dawn and guns go off in the hills,
rough sounds of things being laid out
in the frost: the doe who leaves
her ribs and face behind, the fox
ice-gauzed in his hushed red fur.

*

In seconds breath falters
into the unheard-of. But
what can't be found, that's the sighing
part — rose cloth tattering from the barbed wire,
the footprint left by the country mailbox.
I would coax them back, wait
by the roadsides of the last-seen,
those patches of earth that become years,
one and two and three and

Raised in New Orleans, Katherine Soniat teaches at Virginia Polytechnic Institute and State University, Blacksburg. Her collection *Notes of Departure* won the 1985 Camden Poetry Prize of the Walt Whitman Center for the Arts and Humanities. Her literary prizes include a Bernard DeVoto Scholarship and a Meralmikjen Fellowship in Poetry from the Breadloaf Writers' Conference. Her second full collection, *Breath on the Mirror*, is forthcoming from the University Presses of Florida. She has published poems in *The American Scholar, The Georgia Review, The Kenyon Review, The Laurel Review, Michigan Quarterly Review, The Nation, New Letters, The New Republic, The North American Review, Poetry, Prairie Schooner, The Yale Review*, and many others.